FOLK TALES

The charming retelling of folk tales from other lands will enchant children.

Each book: 32 pages, 6" X 8-1/2", full-color illustrations, grades 2-6

*Publication Date: March 15, 1980

* THE GAZELLE AND THE HUNTER   (0-516-06480-0)
    By Bernice Williams Foley
    Illustrated by Diana Magnuson
A folk tale from Iran in which a hunter traps a beautiful gazelle.

* THE LAD WHO MADE THE PRINCESS LAUGH   (0-516-06481-9)
    By Jane Belk Moncure
    Illustrated by Lois Axeman
A modernized version of the German folk tale, The Golden Goose.

* THE SHOEMAKER AND THE CHRISTMAS ELVES   (0-516-06482-7)
    By Jane Belk Moncure
    Illustrated by Linda Sommers
Much more is made of Christmas in this retelling of the German folk tale,
The Shoemaker and the Elves.

* TALKING TABBY CAT   (0-516-06483-5)
    By Jane Belk Moncure
    Illustrated by Helen Endres
In this version of the French folk tale, Puss in Boots, the cat is a very
feminine tabby cat.

* A WALK AMONG THE CLOUDS   (0-516-06484-3)
    By Bernice Williams Foley
    Illustrated by Mina Gow McLean
A Chinese folk tale of a young man who, by helping a stranger, helps his
village.

*WHY THE COCK CROWS THREE TIMES   (0-516-06485-1)
    By Bernice Williams Foley
    Illustrated by Rondi Marie Anderson
In this version of a Russian folk tale, a cock lends his plumage to a
peacock.

Reinforced Binding

Childrens Press price to Schools and Libraries $5.50

Listed on page 8 of Spring 1980 Checklist/Order Form

A Walk Among Clouds

A FOLK TALE FROM CHINA

by Bernice Williams Foley
illustrated by Mina Gow McLean

ELGIN, ILLINOIS 60120

Distributed by Childrens Press, 1224 West Van Buren Street, Chicago, Illinois 60607.

Library of Congress Cataloging in Publication Data

Foley, Bernice Williams.
 A walk among clouds.

 SUMMARY: A young man's kindness to a stranger ultimately benefits both himself and his Chinese village.
 [1. Folklore—China] I. McLean, Mina Gow. II. Title.
 PZ8.1.F714Th   398.2'1'0951 [B]   79-18295
 ISBN 0-89565-105-X

A Walk
Among
Clouds

A certain Chinese lad named Yo Yun-Hao tried hard to become a scholar. He worked and studied day after day. He even hired a private teacher. But, each time, when the tests came around, although he was bright, he failed them. Soon, all his money for studies was gone.

"I wished to become a scholar," Yo said to himself. "But that is not possible. I must find some other good and useful way to live."

So Yo became a tailor in his small home town. But business was very slow, for there was a terrible drought in that country. No rain had fallen for weeks and weeks. Crops would not grow. People had little money to spend. Yo kept hoping things would get better. Meanwhile, to make enough money, Yo took odd jobs.

5

Within the next six months, Yo made a little profit. He also married a beautiful and gentle bride.

One day, on business, Yo traveled to a
large city. He stopped at an inn for lunch.

As Yo sat at his table, ready to eat his rice and vegetables, he saw a tall man standing in the doorway of the tea house. The man looked lonely, sad, and hungry.

Yo motioned for the tall man to join him at his table.

"Thank you for your kindness," said the tall man. "But I cannot order food. I have no money."

"Please join me anyway," said Yo. He ordered a shoulder of pork and boiled dumplings for the man. It cost him most of the money he had. When the huge platter of food came, the hungry man gobbled it down in a minute.

"Thank you," said the man, when he had finished. "For three years, I haven't had such a good meal."

"Why should a fine fellow like you be hungry?" Yo asked.

"The judgments of the Thunder God may not be talked about," the man said, in a mysterious tone.

"Where do you live?" Yo asked.

"On land I have no home, and on water I have no boat," was the sad reply.

The two men talked on as Yo finished his own food. Just as they were getting ready to leave, it began to rain. Thunder rocked the room.

"We'll have to stay here until it stops raining," Yo said. "I have just enough money to get a room. We can rest while it storms. Then we'll be ready for our journey."

Soon the two men were in a small room with one tiny window. Yo lay down to rest.

Just as Yo was dozing off, the stranger asked, "Yo, would you like to walk among the clouds?"

"Yes," Yo muttered, not really hearing the question.

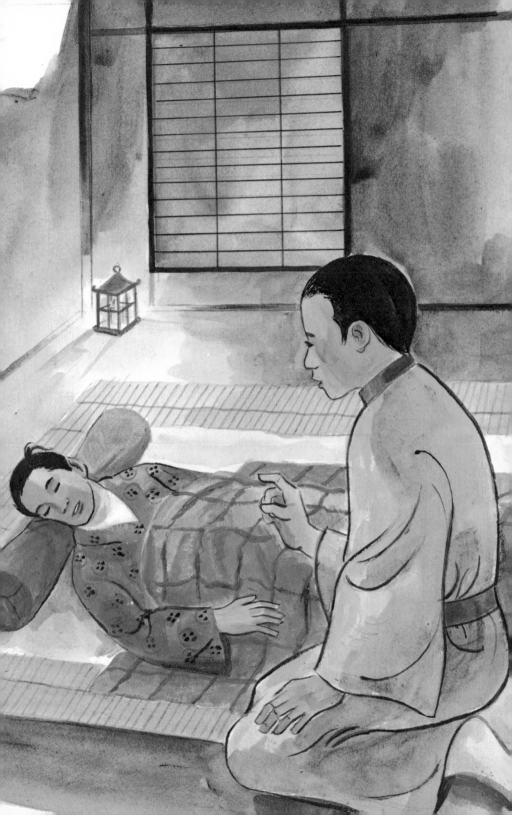

Suddenly, Yo found himself spinning through the air, headed for the storm clouds!

Once among them, Yo discovered that he
could walk on their soft, spongy whiteness.

Yo looked down at the earth. He saw oceans that looked like sheets of silver. He saw large cities filled with houses that looked like small grey beans.

Just then, two dragons came by, pulling a large cart. The cart held a big tank, full of water. Men were ladling out this water into the clouds, so it could become rain and fall to earth. One of these men was Yo's strange friend.

This time, the stranger introduced himself. "My name is Hsai P'ing-tzu," he said. Then he added, "Here, take a ladle and help us bring rain to the clouds."

Yo was pleased to help. He remembered that his own village needed rain. He spoke to a cloud. The cloud promised to fly over Yo's village and spill out its water. So Yo filled the cloud full. Then he helped fill other clouds.

"We are helpers to the God of Thunder," Hsai explained as they worked. "The god became angry with me. To punish me, he sent me to earth. I was there for three years. I could not be freed until someone fed me a generous meal. You did that. Now I am free, and happy to be back in the heavens."

Yo was speechless with surprise.

"You helped me return to my place in the clouds," Hsai continued. "Now I have helped you bring rain to your dry village. It is time for you to return to earth."

25

Hsai handed Yo a rope. "Take hold of this long rope," he said. "Let yourself slide down to your walled town."

Almost at once, Yo was standing in his own village. The village sparkled from a recent rainfall. Yo heard the swish of a rope above his head and saw its end disappearing into the sky.

Yo hurried home. He saw his wife bringing in tubs and buckets of fresh, sweet rainwater. There was a smile of great joy on her face.

"Now our business will be good," she said. "The villagers will grow crops. They will have money to spend."

Later, Yo said to his wife and the villagers, "I brought you the rain."

No one really believed him. But, even so, they wondered.

And as soon as they had money to spend, they gave Yo much business. Yo was a happy man. He had made his life good and useful.

And ever after, he always bought meals for hungry strangers who came to his village.